How to Fix a Lie

How to Fix a Lie

by
Nancy Wilcox Richards

illustrations by
Annabelle Métayer

Scholastic Canada Ltd.
Toronto New York London Auckland Sydney
Mexico City New Delhi Hong Kong Buenos Aires

Scholastic Canada Ltd.
604 King Street West, Toronto, Ontario M5V 1E1, Canada

Scholastic Inc.
557 Broadway, New York, NY 10012, USA

Scholastic Australia Pty Limited
PO Box 579, Gosford, NSW 2250, Australia

Scholastic New Zealand Limited
Private Bag 94407, Botany, Manukau 2163, New Zealand

Scholastic Children's Books
Euston House, 24 Eversholt Street, London NW1 1DB, UK

Library and Archives Canada Cataloguing in Publication
Richards, Nancy Wilcox, 1958-
      How to fix a lie / by Nancy Wilcox Richards ; illustrations by Annabelle
Métayer.

ISBN 978-1-4431-1352-6

      I. Métayer, Annabelle II. Title.

PS8585.I184H696 2012   jC813'.54   C2011-905973-8

6 5 4 3   Printed in Canada 121   13 14 15 16

MIX
Paper from
responsible sources
FSC
www.fsc.org   FSC® C004071

For Kris, who wore that wide-eyed, innocent look on his face every time he tried to sneak a lie past me.

— N.W.R.

Chapter 1

My name is Abby. Well, actually, it's Abigail Jean Fogarty. But nobody calls me that except my mum. And that's only when she's really mad at me. Which is hardly ever. The last time she used my full name was when I accidentally broke the lamp in the living room with my hockey stick. "Abigail Jean Fogarty!" she said. "You know you're not allowed to practise shooting pucks in the house."

That was last winter. Now it's almost summer, and I am counting the days until school is over. There are exactly thirty-two. That means thirty-three days until I head to

Prince Edward Island. I get to spend one whole week in a cottage by the beach — swimming, building sandcastles and having wiener roasts. It will be so much fun! But that's still over a month away. Right now, I have to concentrate on my last few weeks in Grade Three.

Our class will soon be having Pioneer Day. It's one of the best things about Grade Three. Each year, my teacher, Ms Sampson, puts the kids in groups — "pioneer families" she calls them. Everyone gets to dress up in old-fashioned clothes. We spend the whole day doing pioneer activities. I can't wait! It's going to be a blast.

I've been thinking about who might be in my pioneer family. Maybe it will be Lexie or Hannah. Maybe it will even be Stefen. I know there's one kid no one wants to work with — Gracie. I wonder who will get stuck with her.

Gracie's desk is empty. As usual, she is late. She hardly ever comes on time. Ms Sampson asked her one day why she's always so late, but all Gracie did was shrug her shoulders.

I could tell that Ms Sampson was ready to start the day. She just clapped her hands together, jingling her bracelets. That's our signal to stop talking.

"Boys and girls," she began, "it's time for the morning meeting. Everyone head to the carpet, please."

I sat next to Taylor on the carpet. I noticed she was wearing a new bracelet. It wasn't as fancy as Ms Sampson's but I really liked it. It had tiny starfish and shells that dangled back and forth, making a tinkling sound.

"Where'd you get that?" I whispered.

Taylor smiled at me. "I got it this weekend when we were —" Her sentence was interrupted by Ms Sampson.

"Well, girls and boys, it's great to see you all again. Before we start our meeting, does anyone have any weekend news they want to share?" Ms Sampson glanced around the room.

"I went to visit my nanny on the farm," volunteered Soheil. "I got to milk a cow." He wrinkled his face. "It was kind of gross. The milk was really warm." He paused and looked at the rest of us. "But not as gross as helping Nanny shovel horse poop in the stalls!"

Ms Sampson laughed. "I guess that means you don't want to grow up to be a farmer."

Brady waved his hand in the air. "I have news," he shouted out. "I went to a birthday party on Saturday. It was at the bowling alley. I even won a prize."

"I bet you had lots of fun," said Ms Sampson. She looked around. "Does anyone else have something they'd like to share with the cl—"

Bang! The door flew open. Gracie ran into the classroom. Her red hair was messy and her face was red under her freckles. "Sorry I'm late!" she blurted out. "I was helping my mum with . . ."

Ms Sampson stopped her and sighed. "That's okay. Come over and join us for the end of the morning meeting. Maybe tomorrow you can be on time. Now, as I was saying, we have time for a few more stories about our weekends." She looked at Taylor. "Taylor, you had your hand up."

Taylor smiled. "Yesterday I went whale watching. I didn't see any whales but I did see lots of seals and a few dolphins. And I bought this bracelet at the gift store." She wiggled her wrist back and forth, jiggling the tiny charms.

"I went whale watching, too!" Gracie blurted out. "But I saw *hundreds* of whales!" She paused and looked around, making sure she had everyone's attention. "And while I was leaning over the side of the boat to get a better look at a whale, I fell in! The ocean was freezing. The Coast Guard had to come and rescue me. I spent alllllllll night in the water. And that's why I was so late this morning."

Taylor nudged me and rolled her eyes. A few kids snickered.

"That's not true," said Stefen.

"Really?" questioned Ms Sampson. She raised her eyebrows high. I could tell she did not believe Gracie. Not for one single minute.

Gracie nodded her head up and down. She made an X over her chest. "Cross my heart and hope to die if I should ever tell a lie."

"Hmmm," Ms Sampson answered. "Very . . . interesting. We can talk more about that later on." She smiled at us. "Well, now I have some news that I think you'll all be very excited to hear." She paused. "This week we will be starting our unit on pioneers. At the end of the unit, we'll celebrate with Pioneer Day. I hope it will be lots of fun for all of you. And to get us thinking about settlers long ago, I want you to brainstorm all the facts you know about pioneers. Find a partner and let's get started."

Everyone scrambled to find a partner. I wondered who I should pick. Taylor was always lots of fun. But so was Soheil. Maybe I should ask Emma. Making decisions is always so hard. I closed my eyes and thought about it. My eyes snapped open when I heard Ms Sampson's voice.

"I see everyone has a partner," she said. She paused and looked at me. "Well, almost everyone. Abby, you don't have a partner and neither does Gracie. You two girls can pair up."

I sighed. Great, just great. Instead of working with my friends, I'm stuck with someone that nobody likes. The kid no one ever chooses. The best project of the year had just gotten off to a rocky start.

Chapter 2

$\mathcal{G}$racie and I sat on the Comfy Couch. It's the best place to sit. It has three great big, squishy pillows.

"So, what do you know about pioneers?" I asked. I dug my favourite pencil out of my pencil case and got ready to record our facts.

Gracie smiled. "I know zillions of facts!" She began counting them off on her fingers. "First, pioneers took only a few baths every year. They ate almost every part of an animal they killed — even the guts. Ewww. Pretty gross. Annnnnd pioneers . . ."

Gracie continued to rattle off more facts. She talked faster than I could print. Some of the answers seemed like they were true. Some of them were interesting. But some of them seemed crazy, like they were made up. I didn't know which ones were true and which ones weren't.

"Is that really true?" I demanded when Gracie said that pioneers used dried buffalo poop to build a fire.

Gracie nodded her head. "Sure it is. And they used weird things for medicine — like tea made out of tree bark."

I scowled. Drinking tree bark? There was no way that could be true.

Before I could quiz Gracie on her "facts," Ms Sampson signalled for us to stop. She smiled at all of us. "Grade Three, I see that many of you know lots of interesting things about pioneers. A few of you have some of your facts mixed up but I am sure we will learn lots about pioneers over the next few weeks. Right now, I'd like to put you in your pioneer families."

I crossed my fingers and quietly whispered, "Please, please let Taylor or Emma be in my group. Maybe Tyler or Ethan. Anybody but Gracie."

Then Ms Sampson said the words that I had been dreading. "The partner you are working with now will be part of your pioneer family."

I slumped down on the couch. I was stuck with Gracie. The one person nobody wanted to work with. Why did I have such rotten luck? I sighed. I was so busy thinking about working with Gracie that I almost didn't hear

Ms Sampson say, "You can link up with one other group to make your pioneer family."

In a flash, everyone scrambled around the room, choosing their pioneer families. Soheil and Zach raced over to me.

Zach blurted out, "Do you want to be partners with me and —" He stopped speaking and took a long look at Gracie. Then he whispered to me out of the corner of his mouth. "Is Gracie *your* partner?"

I nodded my head.

"We'd love to be partners with you guys," replied Gracie with a big smile. "This will be so much fun!"

I shrugged my shoulders and looked Zach straight in the eye. "We could give it a chance." I smiled weakly. "It might work out fine."

Zach frowned. I knew he didn't want to.

"Please, pretty please," I begged. I crossed my fingers behind my back. "It might even be fun."

Zach scowled at me. "Yeah, right. I don't think . . ."

But before he could finish, Ms Sampson walked toward us. She stopped at Gracie, Zach, Soheil and me. "So, is this pioneer family ready to get started?"

She didn't even wait for an answer before she continued. "First, I want you to think about what job you'd like to have as a pioneer. It might be a good idea if you all choose different jobs." Then Ms Sampson turned and headed over to the next group of kids.

For a moment no one spoke.

"Well," said Soheil, giving a feeble smile, "it's settled. We're a family. We might as well decide what we're all going to be." He paused. "I think I'd like to be a blacksmith. It would be cool making horseshoes! Way more fun than shovelling poop like I did on Saturday."

Zach thought he'd like to be a farmer. "I could plant vegetables. And the best part would be later on when I get to eat them." He smacked his lips together. "Carrots, broccoli, cauliflower — but definitely no Brussels sprouts. I hate Brussels sprouts.

They give me gas. And besides, they smell like stinky feet."

I scratched my head. "I'm not sure what I should be," I admitted. "Maybe I could be a teacher. I don't really know what else women did in the olden days except cook and clean. And I don't want to do that!" I scrunched my nose. "I guess being a teacher could be fun."

"Well, I know for sure what I am going to be," boasted Gracie. She paused, making sure she had everyone's attention. "I'm going to be a fortune teller!"

"A fortune teller?" Zach repeated. I could tell by the tone of his voice he couldn't believe Gracie would pick that for a job. "Who ever heard of a pioneer fortune teller?"

"Yeah," repeated Soheil. "Who ever heard of that? What a dumb idea. What are you going to say? 'Mirror, mirror on the wall, who's the fairest of them all?'"

Gracie's face turned red. She bit her bottom lip. She looked like she was about to say something. Then she turned and walked away from the group.

"Weirdo," muttered Zach, and he shook his head.

I watched Gracie walk over to her seat and sit down. She put her head down on her desk and didn't look at anyone for the rest of the activity.

Chapter 3

Recess, as usual, was lots of fun. I scrambled up the monkey bars and sat on the very top with Zach. I chewed my apple. Juice ran down my chin and dripped onto my t-shirt.

"I don't really want to work with Gracie," I told Zach. "I never know when to believe her. She's always telling me these 'true' stories." I rolled my eyes. "Listen to this one. She said that she's a watermelon-seed-spitting champion! Who ever heard of that? Then she told me she knows how to ride a camel!"

"Really?" Zach laughed. "That's probably not true. But here's something that is true. I know a riddle about a camel. Want to hear it?"

I swallowed a bite of apple. "Sure."

"What did the camel wear when it went into the jungle to hunt?" he asked.

I wrinkled my forehead, concentrating. Thinking. "I don't know. I give up."

Zach laughed and said, "Camel-flage! Get it?"

"I get it." I laughed. "But it's too bad Gracie doesn't 'get it.' Kids would like her more if she wasn't always telling stories. She even said she once went skydiving. Who would ever believe that an eight-year-old went skydiving?"

Zach nodded his head in agreement but I have to admit that I secretly thought skydiving would be awesome. I wondered if it was possible for a kid to do that. Imagine jumping out of a plane, falling through clouds, being up in the sky with the birds. It would be so cool.

"Look over there," said Zach, pointing to the wooden bench.

Gracie was sitting on the bench by herself. She nibbled a slice of watermelon as she watched kids go down the slide and race back up the ladder.

"You going to spit those seeds at me?" Zach yelled to her.

I glared at Zach. It was true that Gracie had bragged about being able to spit a watermelon seed five metres. But it didn't seem right for him to tease her — especially when she looked so sad sitting all alone.

"I think I'm going to take a rest and sit on the bench," I said.

* * *

After recess it was time to work with our pioneer families. I picked up a sheet of paper that Ms Sampson had placed at our table. It read:

Part of Pioneer Day will be spent trading, or bartering. Trading was important to the early settlers. It allowed pioneers to get things that they didn't have but that they needed or wanted. Each member of your pioneer family must decide on something to create, or a service to do, and then trade it for another product or service.

"Hmm," said Soheil, "this is tricky." He frowned.

"I don't know how to make anything," added Zach. "Except my mum says I know how to make a lot of noise!" He laughed.

"I could make cookies," suggested Gracie, "with my mum's help. But I don't know if pioneers ate chocolate-chip cookies. Maybe they ate plain cookies, though — like molasses cookies."

I nodded my head. "Maybe," I agreed. "That's a good idea. We'll have to investigate and see what they baked."

* * *

As soon as I arrived in the classroom the next day, Gracie raced over to me. She had a big smile on her face.

"Guess what I brought to school today," she said.

I studied Gracie closely. Hmmm, nothing in her hands. "I don't know."

Gracie frowned. "Make a guess!" she ordered.

I took a close look at Gracie: purple shirt, black pants, same old sneakers without the laces. "Are you wearing something new?"

"Duh. Does it look like I'm wearing something new?"

I felt my face get warm. "I don't know," I repeated. I paused. I remembered that Ms Sampson had said the class would be learning about pioneer games today. Maybe Gracie brought her favourite game. "Did you bring in a game?"

Gracie let out a loud sigh and rolled her eyes. "No, dummy. Don't you remember anything?" Then she reached over and pinched me on the arm. Hard.

"Ouch!" I cried, rubbing my arm. "That hurt!"

I watched as Gracie stalked back to her seat. What a meanie. I felt like pinching her back. But it would be just my luck that I'd be the one who gets caught. Then *I'd* get the detention, not her.

A moment later, Zach was standing beside me. "I saw her pinch you," he blurted out. He pointed in Gracie's direction. "Want me to tell Ms Sampson?"

I shook my head. "No, I'll be okay."

"So, how come she's so mad?" asked Zach. "I saw you two talking and then she pinched you."

I shook my head again. "I don't know. It's kind of weird. She asked me to guess what she brought to school and when I couldn't figure it out, she got mad." I sighed. "I bet working with our pioneer families won't be any fun at all today."

Chapter 4

Ms Sampson walked over to Zach and me. She had a funny look on her face. "Is everything all right over here?"

I stopped rubbing my arm. I nodded my head up and down. "Fine," I said in a quiet voice.

"Actually," said Zach, "Gracie pinched Abby."

Ms Sampson looked at me. "Is that true?" she asked.

I nodded my head. "And for no reason," I answered. My voice sounded wobbly. My eyes burned. I hoped I wasn't going to cry.

Ms Sampson frowned and looked over at Gracie. Her voice sounded cross when she said, "Gracie, come here please. I need to speak to you. Right now."

Gracie walked over to Ms Sampson. She glared at me.

"I know what you're going to say," she told Ms Sampson. "And yes, I pinched Abby. But she started it. She pinched me first. Because she wanted me to move away from her desk. And all I wanted to do was talk to her. Honest." Her words came out faster and faster. "So I pinched her back. Kind of like self-defence. I know I shouldn't have. It was wrong." She turned and faced me. "I'm really, really sorry. It won't happen again." She faced Ms Sampson and lowered her voice. "I'm sorry, Ms Sampson. It'll never happen again."

I stared at Gracie. I couldn't believe what I was hearing. *I* started it? *I* pinched her?

"That's not true!" I exclaimed. "I did not pinch anyone."

Ms Sampson sighed. I could tell she was not happy. "I think we'll need to talk about this at play time. Right now it's time to start our day. Let's get ready for our morning meeting."

Great. Now I have to miss part of my recess break for something I didn't even do. It just wasn't fair. When Ms Sampson wasn't looking, I turned and stuck my tongue out at Gracie. I didn't even care if I got caught.

I had a hard time concentrating during the morning meeting. All I could think about was Gracie and her lie. It was one thing to make up a story about skydiving. It was another thing to lie and get someone else in trouble. Especially when that someone was me!

During the meeting, Hannah showed us her new sneakers, Zach told us a riddle and Tyler shared that he lost another tooth. It's his tenth one.

"Losing a tooth shows that you are growing up, Tyler. Unfortunately, I lost something this weekend, too," said Ms Sampson. "Not a tooth, of course, but something very valuable." She had a sad look on her face.

"What did you lose?" Soheil asked. "Your purse?"

"No, one of my bracelets. I've searched high and low. I can't find it anywhere. I think it must have somehow fallen off my wrist. But I'm not sure." She sighed. "It was a gift from a very dear friend. She even had my name engraved on the inside. Hopefully I'll find it."

When the morning meeting was over, Ms Sampson talked about pioneer games. I was surprised to learn that many of those same games are still played today — games like tag, hide-and-go-seek, checkers and blind man's bluff. And who would ever think that the first marbles were made of clay? Or that pioneer kids played hopscotch?

While Ms Sampson passed out supplies, Emma said, "Let's get some hula hoops at recess. We could try rolling the hoop, just like pioneers did!"

"That would be fun," I answered, but then I remembered. "But I can't. I have to stay in with Gracie. We have to talk to the teacher."

Emma looked surprised. "Really?"

I nodded. "Yeah, Gracie told Ms Sampson that I pinched her. But I didn't do anything."

"Oh, bummer," whispered Emma. She looked about as sad as I felt. "Well, I'll still get the hoops. Maybe you won't be talking to Ms Sampson too long. I'll wait for you outside."

After learning about pioneer games, it was time for gym. Then it was time for writers' workshop. The morning sailed by and the next thing I knew, the recess bell was buzzing. It was time for our "little chat" with Ms Sampson.

Chapter 5

Ms Sampson sat at her desk. Her hands were folded in her lap. She looked at me, then Gracie.

"Okay, girls," she began, "it seems we have a bit of a problem. A pinching problem, to be exact. Who would like to talk about it first?"

I took a deep breath but before I could say a word, Gracie blurted out, "I did it! I lied. Abby didn't do a thing."

I'm not sure who was more surprised — me, Ms Sampson or Gracie.

"I . . . I . . . I really am sorry." Gracie faced me. "I promise to never pinch you again." A single tear trickled down her cheek. "I don't know why I did it."

Ms Sampson smiled at Gracie. "It takes

a big person to admit when she's made a mistake. Thank you for being honest." She turned to me and said, "You go outside and get some fresh air. Gracie and I are going to talk a bit more."

I didn't wait for Ms Sampson to change her mind. I grabbed my snack and headed outside.

I sat on the wooden bench under the oak tree. I nibbled my cheese and crackers. Kids raced by heading to the monkey bars, swings and slides. I kept watching for Emma. She probably had the hula hoops by now. But where was she?

"Whatcha doin' now?" asked a little voice.

I knew right away who that voice belonged to. Gracie. I didn't feel like answering her. But if I didn't, maybe she'd pinch me again. Even though she promised never to do it again.

I didn't even look at her when I answered. "Waiting for Emma. We're going to play roll the hoop."

"Can I play too?" she asked.

Before I could answer, Gracie thrust her hand out. "Here," she said, "you can try some of my special recess snack if you let me play." She sighed. "I tried to tell you about it this morning. You just couldn't figure it out. Remember?"

I remembered all right. I remembered her tone of voice. I remembered how she had pinched me. I remembered how she accused me of pinching her first. I rubbed my arm and looked at Gracie's snack.

"It's a pioneer snack," Gracie blurted out. "When the settlers ran out of food, sometimes they had to eat bugs." She made a face. "Kind of gross."

I stared at the small, dark brown chunks. "I've never heard of pioneers eating bugs."

"It's ants," Gracie told me. "But my mum and I dipped them in chocolate so they'd taste better."

I peered more closely at the chocolate-covered ants. They looked like chocolate-covered raisins. "Those are not ants!"

Gracie nodded her head. "Yes, they are. I told you, it's emergency pioneer food." She held out her hand. "Try one," she dared.

I studied the chocolate bits. They sure looked like chocolate-covered raisins. But what if they really *were* ants? Eating ants would make a kid sick. Should I take a chance?

I patted my tummy. "I'm full. I just finished my snack."

"Chicken," taunted Gracie.

"Am not!"

"Are too!"

"Am not!"

At that exact moment, Emma plopped down on the bench next to me. She was panting hard. "Sorry it took me so long. I had a hard time finding the hoops." She glanced at me, then at Gracie. "Is everything okay?" she asked.

I didn't answer the question. Instead I said, "Let's go play." I didn't invite Gracie to join us.

Chapter 6

The next day, I tried to avoid Gracie as much as possible. It was pretty hard to do, especially since we're in the same pioneer family.

The whole class was working on the Internet, researching facts about pioneers. I found out a few more things I didn't know.

I thought it was neat that because pioneers didn't have fridges, they dried their meat so it could be stored longer and still be safe to eat. The dried meat was called beef jerky. And it was also pretty cool that they didn't have glass. Windows were made of greased paper.

After we worked on the Internet, it was time for music. It's one of my favourite subjects. Today we were learning about famous musicians like Mozart and Beethoven. Sometimes a band comes into our class. Last week "Neon Highway," a band from Malone Bay, put on a show for the whole school.

As soon as I walked through the door to the music room, I noticed flowers on the teacher's desk.

"I like your roses," I told Mrs. Rock.

"Thank you," replied Mrs. Rock. "It's my birthday today."

"It's my birthday, too!" piped in Gracie.

Mrs. Rock looked surprised. "Really? Well, happy birthday!"

She faced the rest of the class. "Boys and

girls, it's Gracie's birthday." She played a few notes on the piano and began to sing, "Happy birthday to you, happy birthday . . ." The class joined in. I stared at Gracie. What a strange coincidence. Gracie has the same birthday as Mrs. Rock. Funny she didn't mention it earlier.

"Is it really your birthday today?" I quizzed her.

Gracie's head bobbed up and down. "Yup," she paused, "and . . . and . . . you're invited to my party. Today . . . right after school."

* * *

Part of me didn't believe that it was her birthday. But another part of me really wanted to believe that she wouldn't lie about something like that. I decided that I would take a chance and trust that she was telling the truth.

Birthday parties are my absolute most-favourite thing. This would be the tenth party I was invited to this year. It took me quite a while to convince my mum that I really *was* invited to Gracie's house for her birthday party. Then, we had to rush to the mall to buy a present. We have this rule in our house about buying gifts. I have to pay for half; my mum pays for the other half, plus the taxes.

I spent a long time trying to decide what to buy. Should I buy a stuffed animal? Maybe a new game? I didn't really know what Gracie liked. Finally, I picked out an artist gift pack. It even had special coloured pencils that you dip in water to make really cool colours. I kind of wished I could buy the artist set for myself. It cost me a whole week's allowance. I sure hoped Gracie would like it.

I felt a little nervous when I rang the doorbell to Gracie's house. She told me she lives just three houses away from the school, at 59 White Spruce Lane. So it wasn't hard to find at all. I waited for her to answer the door. Finally, after what seemed like a long time, the door opened. A woman with long, red hair tied back with a bow smiled at me. She had brown eyes just like Gracie's. I was pretty sure it was her mother.

"Can I help you?" she asked me.

"I'm here for the party," I said. "Sorry I'm so late. Gracie just told me about it today at school." I thrust the present in her direction. It was wrapped in blue paper with a silver bow.

"Party?" repeated the woman. She stared at the gift. "What party? There's no party here."

"Maybe I have the wrong house," I stammered. "Does . . . does . . . Gracie Tanner live here?"

"Yes, but my goodness, it isn't her birthday today. Her birthday was last month."

At that moment, I heard running footsteps inside the house. They came closer and closer. In a few seconds, a panting Gracie stood next to her mother. She grinned when she saw me.

"Abby, what are you doing here?" she asked. Then she looked down at the present in my hand. Her eyes got wide. "Uh-oh," she gulped. She looked up at her mother, then back at me. "Oops." She said it so softly I barely heard it.

Gracie's mother glared at her. "What exactly is going on here?" she demanded. "Did you tell this girl it was your birthday?"

Tears came to Gracie's eyes. I felt sorry for her. But not as sorry as I felt for me. I had just spent the last of my allowance on her birthday gift. And there wasn't even a birthday!

Gracie nodded her head up and down. "Sorry," she whispered. Then she ran off down the hallway.

Chapter 7

"So," I told Lexie the next morning at school, "there was no party. And I wasted the last of my allowance on a stupid gift. So much for giving Gracie a chance."

Lexie looked sympathetic. "I bet she was in big trouble after you left. My parents would ground me for a year if I did something like that." She grinned at me. "But if you look on the bright side, you now own some really cool art supplies."

"That's true," I agreed and smiled. I looked around the room. There was no sign of Gracie. Her seat was empty. She was late again. "I wonder where Gracie is," I said.

"If I were her, I'd be too embarrassed to

come to school today," Lexie answered. "I wouldn't want to show my face."

No sooner were the words out of Lexie's mouth than the door opened and in walked Gracie. She kept her head bowed low, eyes on the floor, and scurried into her seat.

"Good morning, Gracie," Ms Sampson said. "I heard that yesterday was a special day. How's the birthday girl today?"

Gracie's face turned a bright shade of red. I couldn't hear what she told the teacher but it sounded like she said she was feeling sick. Part of me thought that I'd feel sick, too, if I got caught in a big lie like she did. But another part of me felt a little bit bad for her. Maybe she hadn't celebrated her real birthday. There had to be a reason behind all of her stories. I didn't have time to think about the birthday girl anymore because just then Ms Sampson starting digging some pioneer things out of a box.

"Girls and boys," began Ms Sampson, "these are slates. Years ago, children used them in school. They practised their math, learned to write and a whole lot more. This morning, I'd like for you and your pioneer family to practise writing your names on the slate." She handed out pieces of chalk to everyone.

I headed to the back of the room. Soheil, Zach and Gracie were already there waiting for me. This was going to be fun. In my best cursive, I carefully wrote *A-b-b-y*. I peeked at Gracie's slate. She had already written her name, plus the words "Malone Bay Public School" on her slate. She was pretty good using the chalk. When she saw me watching her, she said, "I'm used to writing on a slate. We have a humongous one right in our kitchen."

I sighed. Didn't Gracie ever learn? Even after lying about her birthday, she was still making up stories.

"I bet," said Soheil.

"Sure you do," chimed in Zach. I watched as he angrily wrote *L-I-A-R* on his slate and held it up for her to see.

Gracie's eyes widened and filled with tears. Then she clutched her belly and moaned. "I feel sick. I think I'm going to throw up."

Zach snickered. I knew he didn't believe her. Neither did I. It was just another story.

Ms Sampson approached our group. "Is everything okay?" she asked.

"Gracie says she feels sick," Soheil explained.

Ms Sampson took a long look at Gracie. She didn't say anything. Then she noticed the word "LIAR" on Zach's slate. Ms Sampson frowned at him. Quickly, Zach erased his slate. I knew the last thing he wanted was a detention. He loves playing outdoors.

"I wonder if your tummy ache has something to do with not getting along with the kids in your group?" Ms Sampson looked directly at Zach.

"No," whispered Gracie, "I really *do* feel sick." She moaned and clutched her belly again.

"Liar, liar, your pants are on fire," Zach chanted under his breath. He said it low enough that Ms Sampson couldn't hear him.

"Stop it," I whispered to Zach.

I eyed Gracie. Her face WAS getting whiter by the minute.

Ms Sampson seemed about to say something when Gracie let out an extra-loud moan. And then, "Blaaagh!" She threw up. It was everywhere. Some of it landed on Zach's slate. Most of it landed on Soheil's shoes. I tried hard not to look at it. But I could see there were brown chunks of something disgusting. And then I felt a wave of sadness come over me. Gracie had said she was sick. None of us, me included, had believed her.

"Ms Sampson," I volunteered, "I'll take Gracie to the washroom and help her get cleaned up."

Ms Sampson smiled at me. "I'd appreciate that," she said.

Soon after that, Gracie went home. She didn't come back for the next two days.

Chapter 8

The rest of the week zipped by. We learned lots more interesting pioneer facts. I thought it was neat that soap used to be made from wood ashes and animal fat. But when Ms Sampson said the whole family shared the same bath water, I thought that was gross. She explained that the father usually got to take his bath first. Next came the mother, then the oldest child after her. It kept going until the youngest kid got to take a bath last. In the same water! Since I'm the youngest in our house, that would mean four people would have a bath ahead of me. I'd have to take my bath after my brother. He's always digging in the dirt. By the time I'd get in the water, it would be black. There would probably be bits of dirt and worms in the water. Disgusting.

"Boys and girls," began Ms Sampson, "I want to remind you that it will soon be Pioneer Day." She looked around the room. "Each one of you needs to think about something you can bring to trade, or barter, that day. You might bake bread and trade it for wool. You might bring in a bit of maple syrup and barter that for a pair of knitted socks. It's totally up to you. Be creative." She smiled. "Now, it's time for us to try a new pioneer activity." She dug in the box and began pulling out supplies. "Today we'll be using these." She waved some feathers around. "Does anyone want to make a guess what we might be doing?"

"Are we making a craft?" guessed Gracie.

Ms Sampson shook her head.

"Are we going to read a book about birds?" asked Taylor.

"No," answered Ms Sampson. She held up a bottle with something dark in it. "We'll also be using this. It's ink."

"We're going to write by dipping the feather in the ink!" blurted out Emma.

"That's right," said Ms Sampson. She showed us how to carefully dip the feather in the ink and write on the paper. "Let's get started, shall we?"

Learning to write using a quill and ink is pretty messy work. Every time I dipped my feather into the ink, it dripped all over my paper. There were splotches everywhere.

We were supposed to practise our multiplication tables. I think Soheil was drawing instead. And Zach had more ink on his hands than on the paper. I looked over at Gracie's work.

"You're good at that," I told her.

"Thanks," she said. "It's fun to do." She stopped writing numbers and looked at me. "It's been fun being in your pioneer family. Well . . . most of the time." She continued, "But I still haven't figured out what I can make so I can do some trading with the other pioneers. What are you going to trade for Pioneer Day?"

"I don't know how to make much of anything," I admitted. "I can knit a little. So I am thinking about making a pot holder."

"I'm going to make butter," Soheil volunteered. "All I need is cream and a jar and muscles." He laughed and flexed his arm. "I want to trade my butter for some beef jerky."

Zach said, "I've got mine done already. I made a fishing rod. I used a stick for the pole and a paper clip for the hook."

"I don't think pioneers had paper clips." Soheil laughed.

Zach shrugged. "It's the best I could do. What are you going to trade, Gracie?"

Gracie looked worried. She chewed on a hangnail. "I'm not sure. I'm not good at making things. I was thinking . . . I might . . . just might . . . trade in a real pioneer person." She looked down at her lap.

Trade a person? Who ever heard of that? This had to be the craziest story yet. I could feel my temper bubbling. I thought about all the things Gracie had insisted were true: falling overboard when she was whale watching; eating chocolate-covered ants; her fake birthday. I remembered her telling me she used to live in a jungle. And that her aunt was a real princess.

It was like I couldn't stop the words from exploding out of my mouth: "There are no pioneers anymore!" I yelled. "And you definitely can't trade them! What's the matter with you? All you do is lie. No wonder no one wants to take a chance and be your friend!"

I was sorry the minute the words were out of my mouth. Zach and Soheil gaped at me. Gracie stared at me, her mouth opening and closing. Her hands were balled into tight fists on her lap.

"I shouldn't have said that," I stammered. "I'm sorry. Maybe I . . . I could help you . . . figure out what to make." My voice trailed off.

"Never mind," Gracie whispered. "Just never mind." She picked up her quill and began writing.

Chapter 9

On Tuesday, we learned how to card wool using special brushes. On Wednesday, we baked bread. Thursday, we went to the Family Studies Room. Usually only Junior High kids are allowed in there. But today we were using the room to make stew. Ms Sampson told us we'd eat the stew tomorrow, on Pioneer Day. Each pioneer family had a pile of cut-up vegetables to wash: potatoes, carrots, turnips, celery and parsnips.

"I don't like parsnips," Zach complained.

"Me neither," said Gracie, sticking out her tongue.

I shrugged my shoulders. I wasn't too keen on them either. "I guess we'll have to pick out all the stuff we don't like."

We washed vegetables. And then we washed more vegetables. And when my vegetable pile was almost gone, Ms Sampson gave me even more vegetables. Finally after what seemed like hours of washing, we were ready to cook the stew.

While the stew was bubbling away, Ms Sampson told us a story about a famous pioneer, Emily Stowe. "She had a couple of jobs. First she was a teacher. Then she decided she wanted to be a doctor," explained Ms Sampson. "But she was not allowed to go to medical school. Can anyone guess why?"

I raised my hand. "Is it because she didn't have enough money?"

Ms Sampson shook her head.

"Maybe her report card wasn't very good," suggested Lexie.

Again Ms Sampson shook her head. She studied us for a moment and then she said, "Emily Stowe didn't get into medical school because she was . . . a girl."

"That's not fair," I blurted out. I looked around the room. Heads were nodding up and down.

"Yeah, that's not fair," agreed Gracie.

"Not fair."

"Not fair."

"You're right, Grade Three. It wasn't fair," agreed Ms Sampson. "But the good news is, Emily Stowe didn't give up and eventually did become a doctor. And today we have lots of female doctors." She smiled. "Now, while the stew is cooking, I'd like to read you this story about her." Ms Sampson began reading. I had a hard time concentrating.

The stew was starting to smell really good, even if it did have parsnips in it. It made my stomach growl. It didn't growl just a little. It growled a lot. And it wasn't a tiny little noise either. It sounded like a lion lived in my belly. Gracie was sitting next to me. After the third roar, she looked over at me and started to laugh. She put her hands over her mouth so she wouldn't make a sound. But her shoulders were shaking. Then she reached into her pocket and pulled out something small. It was in her fist.

Gracie held her fist under the table and tapped me. "Here," she whispered. She unfolded her fist to show me a tiny foil-covered candy.

My eyes widened. What if Ms Sampson caught me eating during class time? My belly rumbled again. I bit my lip. Should I? Or shouldn't I? I reached under the table and took the candy. Very carefully, keeping the candy hidden, I peeled off the wrapper.

"Thanks," I whispered, and popped it in my mouth.

Gracie smiled at me. "You're welcome."

Chapter 10

Finally the day that I had been waiting for arrived. It was Pioneer Day! It felt like it took forever to get here. Even though it was pouring outside, I didn't care. Nothing was going to spoil today.

Ms Sampson had suggested that everybody dress like pioneers for the day. I had a tough time deciding what to wear. Should I dress up like a doctor? Maybe I should be a farmer. In the end, I decided to dress up as a teacher. I wore a long skirt, a plain cotton blouse, a shawl and a bonnet. I couldn't wait to see what everyone else was wearing.

I didn't have to wait long.

The first person I saw when I got to Malone Bay Public School was Ms Sampson. She laughed when she saw me. "I guess you and I both decided to dress as pioneer teachers!"

I looked at her outfit: long skirt, plain blouse, shawl and bonnet. The only difference was that she was holding a slate.

I laughed.

The next person I saw was from my pioneer family. It was Soheil. He held up a rusty horseshoe. It looked heavy. "Guess who I am," he said.

I knew right away. "You're a blacksmith," I answered.

He grinned. "Right. Got any horses that need new shoes?"

Then I spotted Zach. He was wearing overalls and a large straw hat. He was chewing on a piece of hay. It was pretty easy to guess that he was a farmer.

I looked around the room for Gracie. As usual, she was late. How could she always be late? Especially since she only lived three houses away from the school. I couldn't figure that out. I didn't get the chance to think about it for too long because Ms Sampson clapped her hands together to get our attention.

"Class," she began, "welcome to Pioneer Day. We have lots of fun things planned for our day, including a delicious pioneer lunch. So we should begin. I think we should start with trading our supplies, or things you've made." She walked over to a table. "I made these sugar cookies last night. I'd like to trade a half-dozen of them for something else. Do I have anyone who wants to barter?"

"How about some butter?" suggested Soheil.

"I've got biscuits," yelled Lexie.

"I'll trade one of my potholders for a full dozen of your cookies," I volunteered.

"A full dozen," Ms Sampson repeated. She tapped her finger against her chin. "You drive a hard bargain, Abby. But it's a deal." She placed twelve sugar cookies on a paper plate and put them on my desk. I gave her one of my potholders. It was the best one. It didn't have any holes in it from dropped stitches and the sides were pretty even.

It was fun trading our stuff. Zach traded his homemade fishing rod for a whirligig. Soheil traded his butter for some strawberry jam.

I still had two potholders left. I wasn't
sure what I wanted to trade them for. There
was pemmican made with cranberries and
something else. But I couldn't tell what the
other ingredients were. I took a sniff. Yuck.
Disgusting. No pemmican for me. There were
Lexie's biscuits. They looked really good —
big, fat and golden brown. Emma had dipped

candles. And Max had seeds from last fall's garden. I thought the seeds would be a good trade. I could grow pumpkins and zucchinis. That would be fun!

"I'll trade you this for some seeds," I suggested. I held up a potholder.

Max looked at the potholder. He poked his finger through a hole. "What would I do with a potholder?" he asked. "And it has two holes in it."

"You could give it to your mum for a birthday gift. Mums love these kinds of things." I crossed my fingers behind my back.

"My mum's birthday isn't until November," he replied.

"Think of it as early birthday shopping. You won't have to worry about forgetting her special day."

Max looked doubtful. "Well . . . I guess."

So then I had a dozen sugar cookies and some pumpkin and zucchini seeds. I had one potholder left to trade. What should I get?

I walked from table to table looking at all

of my choices. I was halfway through making another trade when the classroom door banged open. The class turned and stared.

"Sorry I'm late," a breathless Gracie panted. "I couldn't find my boots." She pointed at her feet. Muddy green boots left tracks all over the floor.

"Just come in," sighed Ms Sampson. "We're still bartering. What did you bring to trade?"

"Well . . ." Gracie began. She twisted her hands nervously. "There's a little problem."

Chapter 11

*A*ll of a sudden the room went really quiet. Everyone stopped their trading. Twenty pairs of eyes focused on Gracie. She cleared her throat and in her quietest voice whispered, "I don't have anything to trade."

"Oh," replied Ms Sampson. "Did you forget that it was Pioneer Day?"

"Well, I did have something to trade." Gracie paused. She seemed to be searching for the right words to say. Probably another story. "Actually not some*thing*," she admitted. "Some*one*."

Ms Sampson stared at Gracie. "Did you say *someone*? *Someone*?" She frowned. "That's not really possible. You can't trade a person." She sighed again. "Oh, Gracie, just come in and get ready for the day."

Gracie's lower lip quivered. She walked over to her desk and began fiddling with something inside. It looked like another candy wrapped in foil — the kind she had shared with me.

The rest of the class went back to trading. I stared at Gracie. Slowly I walked over to her desk.

"If you don't have anything to trade, you can have this." I thrust my last potholder at her. "I knit three of them. And I've already traded two of them for other things." I held up a bag of seeds.

A tear ran down her face. "Thanks," she sniffled. "But you don't get it. I really did have someone to trade. I guess no one believes a word I say anymore."

Part of me wanted to say, "Well, what did you expect?" I mean, you can't make up stories time after time and then expect others to believe you. But another part of me felt sorry for Gracie. I don't think she meant to be mean. In fact, sometimes she was sort of funny. Like the time she showed the class how to make monkey sounds and peel a banana without using your hands. But sometimes she had a problem with telling the truth.

I took a deep breath and thought about what to say. I chose my words carefully.

"Did you remember that we were supposed to *make* something to trade? Ms Sampson said we could even offer a service. We could do something a pioneer would do. Like trade an hour of weeding in a garden for some vegetables." I paused and watched as a tear dripped off Gracie's chin and landed with a plop on the floor. And then in my softest voice I said, "I don't see how you can trade a real person."

Gracie stared at me. "It's my great-great-Grandma Stella. She lives with us and she's one hundred years old. Honest." Gracie placed her finger on her chest and traced an X. "Cross my heart and hope to die if I should ever tell a lie."

I thought about that. Could it be true? I wondered if a one-hundred-year-old person was a pioneer.

"Grandma Stella moved in with us a few years ago. I help my mum take care of her. Every morning I help her get dressed. I help sit her at the table. I even get her tea ready. Grandma Stella remembers when *her* grandmother lived at her house. And she was a real pioneer from Sherbrooke," explained Gracie. "So, since Grandma Stella is really old, and she lived with a real pioneer, it's like she's practically a pioneer, too!"

Gracie paused and looked at me. I could tell by the look on her face she wanted me to understand.

"And I know I can't really trade Grandma Stella but I can trade something she does. Just like Ms Sampson said we could do. I was going to . . ."

Gracie didn't get the chance to finish her

sentence because there was a knock at the door. I watched as Gracie practically flew across the room to answer the door. I have never seen anyone run so fast. She flung open the door and there stood her mother with a tiny and very wrinkly little old lady in a wheelchair.

"Grandma Stella! Mum! You made it!" Gracie shrieked.

Everyone stopped their trading and stared at the two visitors.

Gracie turned and faced the class. "Hey, everybody! I can start my trading now. My great-great-Grandma Stella is here!"

Chapter 12

Ms Sampson quickly walked toward the door. I think she looked more surprised than anyone. But I felt really puzzled. I still didn't get how you could trade a person.

Gracie hugged her mum. "You made it! I was so worried." She faced Ms Sampson. "I can start my trading now."

"Okaaaay," answered Ms Sampson. She looked very confused. "But what is it exactly that you are trading?"

Gracie smiled. "My Grandma Stella. Well, not her — but something she does. She does a pioneer pastime."

"Really?" Ms Sampson answered. She was looking more confused by the minute.

I wondered what Grandma Stella could do.

She was so little. And SO old. Plus she was in a wheelchair. She looked like she was a million years old.

"Yes," Gracie said. "Grandma Stella is . . ." she paused, "a fortune teller! She can read your fortune in tea leaves." She looked around the room. "Who wants to make a trade and have their fortune told?"

"Cool!"

"Sweet!"

"Me first!"

I helped Gracie pass out tiny white cups. Her mother poured a little tea from a thermos in each cup. Bits of tea leaves floated on the top and settled to the bottom of the cup.

"How about if I start?" Ms Sampson suggested. "I'll trade some of my sugar cookies for my fortune."

Grandma Stella smiled. In a quivery voice she answered, "I love sugar cookies. Excellent idea, Donna . . . er . . . I mean, Ms Sampson."

Now that was definitely weird. How did Grandma Stella know Ms Sampson's first name? I watched Ms Sampson drink her tea, leaving bits of leaves in the bottom of her cup.

"I see that you love your job," Grandma Stella began. She stared intently into the bottom of the cup. "And soon you will receive a package. Something you want." She smiled at Ms Sampson. "But, I have to say, you really must watch that cat of yours. He has already ruined one of your chairs with all his crazy scratching."

Ms Sampson stared at Grandma Stella. "How . . . how . . ." she stammered. "How did you know that?"

Grandma Stella smiled back at her. "I have my ways," she answered mysteriously.

I watched as kid after kid lined up to have their fortunes told. First Lexie had a turn. Then Zach. So far Gracie had collected bannock, biscuits, wool mittens and even a cowbell. "Now is there anyone else left who would like to have their fortune told?" asked Grandma Stella. She looked around the classroom. Her gaze settled on her great-great-granddaughter. "What about you, Gracie? Drink your tea. Then I'll take a peek at your leaves."

Obediently, Gracie drank her tea and thrust her cup into Grandma Stella's hand. Grandma Stella stared into the bottom of the cup. She cleared her throat and frowned.

"I see you like to tell stories, maybe too many stories," she began.

A few kids laughed. Gracie's face turned red.

"But this is about to change," she predicted. "After today you will believe more in yourself and all the special things you can do." She paused and studied the leaves some more.

"I see that your friends don't know that you once won the watermelon-seed-spitting contest. And you didn't tell them about riding a camel last summer." She smiled at Gracie. "I think they would find those stories most interesting."

I glanced over at Soheil. He looked as surprised as me. So did the rest of the class. Gracie actually *had* ridden a camel. That was so cool! Then I looked over at Gracie. Her smile stretched from ear to ear.

"Did you tell them about the time you rescued a trapped puppy? Or that last summer you found a rare dinosaur fossil?"

Gracie shook her head.

"I think you need to share these wonderful stories. They are amazing — just like you," said Grandma Stella. "But, please," she paused and smiled, "no more pretend stories." She studied the teacup one last time. "And, my dear, I predict the best news of all. I see some new friends, from this room, in your very near future."

Chapter 13

Grandma Stella left after that. Then it was time for our pioneer lunch. I couldn't wait to taste the stew, even if it did have parsnips in it. There was homemade bread, and for dessert, an apple crisp. Just thinking about it made my mouth water.

"Girls and boys," began Ms Sampson, "our Pioneer Day is continuing right on schedule. I hope you are enjoying it as much as I am. I think you all did a wonderful job trading today. There were definitely a few surprises." She looked over at Gracie and smiled. "And I know our lunch is going to be delicious."

Heads nodded up and down.

"Let's get ready to enjoy our pioneer meal."

I ate two bowls of stew. I even ate the

parsnips. They were okay, but definitely not my favourite veggie. Zach ate four bowls of stew. After that he said he was too full to eat any of the apple crisp. So I ate his. It was the best lunch ever. We all took turns washing our dishes in a dishpan, just like the pioneers did. No dishwashers, that's for sure.

When all of our mess had been tidied away, we headed outside to play. Leapfrog was fun.

Playing with the marbles would definitely take more practice. But the best game was the three-legged race. Gracie and I were partners. We didn't win but it was close.

After recess, it was time to wrap up our Pioneer Day.

"This was such a great day," began Ms Sampson. "Would anyone like to share their favourite part of the project?"

Twenty hands shot into the air. Ms Sampson smiled. "Let's start with —"

There was a knock at the door. Ms Sampson opened the door. No one was there. The hallway was empty. But a small brown box sat on the floor. Ms Sampson frowned.

"That's odd," she murmured. She picked up the box and brought it in to the classroom.

"Who's it for?" yelled Stefen.

"Let's check," answered Ms Sampson. Silently she read the tag. She had a surprised look on her face. "Why, it's for me," she said. "But what could it be?"

"Open it!"

Slowly Ms Sampson unwrapped the brown box and took off the lid.

"I don't believe it," she whispered.

I stared at Ms Sampson. "What is it? Can you tell us?"

Ms Sampson reached into the box and began pulling out wads of tissue paper. A few pieces fluttered to the floor. Then she slowly pulled out . . . a bracelet. I knew right away who it belonged to.

"This is the bracelet that I lost a few days ago. I thought I'd never see it again. Who could have returned it to the school? And how did the person know it belonged to me?" She slipped the bracelet on her arm and smiled. She looked really happy.

I pointed to a piece of paper that had fallen on the floor. "I think that's a note," I said.

Ms Sampson picked up the note and read:

Dear Ms Sampson,

I found this bracelet on the sidewalk. Because your name was engraved on the inside, I am able to return it to you. It looks like it's a pretty special piece of jewellery.

Robert John

P.S. I fixed the broken clasp. Hopefully you won't lose it again!

Gracie yelled out, "It's just like Grandma Stella said. She said you'd get a special package. This must be it!"

Ms Sampson sat down. "Amazing," she said. "I don't understand how Grandma Stella knew. . . ." She shook her head. "Well, I guess that's it for the day, class." She was still shaking her head as we filed out the door. "See you on Monday."

Chapter 14

Ms Sampson was still thinking about Grandma Stella on Monday. I could tell because it's the first thing she talked about. She started off our morning meeting saying, "That tea reading has to be one of the highlights of Pioneer Day for me." She looked at the rest of us. "Would anyone like to share their favourite part about our pioneer activities? We never did get around to that on Friday."

"I liked learning about the pioneer games," said Soheil. "Making shadow animals was pretty neat."

"I liked eating the food," said Zach, "especially the bread with homemade butter."

"That was my favourite part, too!" said

Gracie. "Plus, I really liked it when I shared my chocolate-covered ants." She stopped and looked at me. She lowered her voice. "Actually, I have a confession to make." She glanced about the room. "They weren't chocolate-covered ants. They were just . . . raisins."

I smiled at Gracie. Raisins. I knew that's what they had been. But I was glad she had admitted it. I looked around at the rest of the kids. They were smiling, too.

Gracie took a deep breath. "Truthfully," she admitted, "the best part was having my fortune told. And finding out that I'm kind of interesting."

Ms Sampson smiled. "Yes, you sure have done some *very* interesting things, Gracie. I'd love to find out about how you discovered a dinosaur fossil."

"I want you to teach me how to ride a camel!" yelled Zach.

"Well," answered Gracie, "in order to do that I'd need a camel. And my camel is . . ." She paused and looked directly at Zach.

"Actually, I don't have a camel. So showing you how to ride one would be hard to do. But I can teach all of you one thing . . . if you want."

"Sure," I answered. "What is it?"

Gracie reached into her pocket and pulled out a clear bag. It was filled with seeds.

Not pumpkin seeds. Not zucchini seeds. Watermelon seeds. "I can teach you how to spit watermelon seeds really far."

Ms Sampson laughed. "Sounds like we need to go out on the playground for this activity."

"Let's go!"

"Cool!"

I walked beside Gracie as we headed out for the playground.

"You know," I said, "I never got a chance to tell my favourite part about Pioneer Day." I smiled at Gracie. "I thought the best part was having your great-great-grandma come in. Reading the tea leaves was lots of fun. But even better than that was finding out about all the things you can do. I really want to find out how you rescued a puppy."

"Really? Do you mean it?" asked Gracie. She looked surprised and happy. And that made me feel good.

I thought about giving Gracie another chance. Kind of like a fresh start. Before I could change my mind, I said, "Sure. Maybe some day after school, you could come to my house and tell me all about it."

Gracie smiled. "I'd like that."

"You know," I continued, "I think that more of your fortune is also going to come true."

Gracie looked puzzled. "More of my fortune?" she repeated. "What part is that?"

I grinned and said, "The part about you making a new friend."

Also by
Nancy Wilcox Richards

- How to Tame a Bully

- How to Outplay a Bully

- How to Handle a Bully

- How to Be a Friend